Animal Hospital

Script adaptation by Loren Zeisler

GRANADA
MEDIA

One morning, Tom and Vicky
were playing Animal Hospital
in their tree-house.

They had already bandaged some of their teddies and
decided that Hippleottomus would be their next patient.
'Poor Hippleottomus,' said Tom.

'You'll soon be better,' said Vicky, 'but we'll have to make sure you take your medicine every day.'

Suddenly, they heard Grandad calling them from the ground below.

'Hello, Grandad,' said Vicky, leaning out of the window with Hippleottomus in her arms.

'Oh dear!' said Grandad. 'What's happened to Hippopotamus?'

'Hippleottomus!' Vicky corrected him.
'She's got a bad case of galloping lumps,' said Tom.
'But don't worry, Grandad. She's going to get better.'
'Look, Tom,' said Vicky. 'There's our next patient.'

She pointed down to the doghouse where Flossie the cat was having a snooze.

They hurried down the ladder and stood looking at Flossie. Tom said, 'I think she might have galloping lumps, too!'

'Oh no,' said Vicky. 'Cats don't get galloping lumps. That's what hippleottomuses get. Cats get flea fever.'

'Flossie hasn't got fleas!' protested Tom.

'She might not have fleas,' Vicky told him, 'but that doesn't mean to say she can't get flea fever.'

'Anyway,' said Tom, 'whatever it is, we'll have to do something quickly or ...' He suddenly noticed that Flossie had disappeared. '... Oh. She must have got better all of a sudden.'

Meanwhile, under the bridge, the frogs were practising dives for the Froglympics.

'Watch this, Fred,' said Bert. 'A double-back-twisted-pike somersault.'

'Oh no!' said Fred. 'Oh no, no, no. Where is it?'

'Where's what?' asked Bert.

'This pike!' said Fred. 'You know what Squidge said about pikes. "The pike is a greedy fish that lurks in a clump of weed waiting for an unsuspecting frog to come along, and then it eats the frog up, bones and all." I don't want to end up as a pike's dinner!'

'Fred,' said Bert.

Fred continued, 'No thank you very much, if it's all the same to ...'

'FRED!' shouted Bert.

'What?'

'It isn't that kind of pike,' said Bert. 'It's a sort of dive. Watch. And learn.'

Bert started to run around, building up to his amazing
dive, but at the last minute he slipped and fell flat on his back
at the edge of the pond.

'Hurray!' cheered Fred. 'Great dive, Bert! Brilliant! But
aren't you supposed to go into the water when you're diving?'

'Aaaggh!' moaned Bert.

Tom and Vicky watched as Kevin the dog sniffed a flower and started to sneeze madly.

'Poor Kevin,' sighed Tom.

'It looks like dog flu,' Vicky said.

'I think we'll have to bandage him up and put him to bed,' added Tom.

They took Kevin up to the
Animal Hospital and started
to put bandages on him.

But then Kevin decided that he didn't want to play this game.
He leapt down from the tree-house, trailing his bandages, and
hid in the garden.

Tom and Vicky looked everywhere for him – the greenhouse, the shed, even in the runner beans!

Eventually they found him hiding under the wheelbarrow. But when they lifted it up, Kevin dashed away and they had to chase him all around the garden.

He was so quick that they couldn't catch him, and finally they gave up and went looking for other patients.

When Kevin ran over the bridge, one of his bandages fell off and landed near the frogs. Bert was still lying on his back.

'It's all your fault!' Bert told Fred. 'I might as well wave goodbye to the Froglympics. I'll never be the same again.'

' 'Course you will, Bert,' said Fred. 'All you need's a spot of bandaging.'

He fetched the bandage that Kevin had dropped.

'Look!' he said. 'Now, where does it hurt?'

'Well, here,' said Bert, pointing at his upper leg. 'And here.'
He pointed further down. 'And ...'

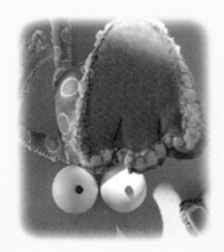 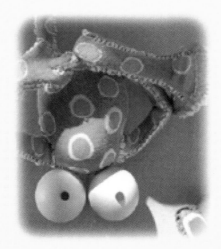

Fred started to wrap the bandages around him.
'Right,' said Bert. 'Fred, I think that's ... whoa! That's
enough! Stop it! It's only my leg that's ... mmmffnnngg!'

Fred had bandaged him so completely that only Bert's eyes were showing. He looked like an Egyptian mummy!

Bert was furious. He started staggering about, trying to get his hands on Fred. Unfortunately, he lost his balance just at the edge of the pond. There was a loud 'plop' as he fell in head-first.

Tom and Vicky bandaged Lotty the chicken and her egg, their pet tortoise Flash, Harry the spider, and lots of other creatures they found in the garden. Then they heard a strange 'ZZzzzz' noise.

'What's that?' said Vicky.

Tom giggled. 'Sounds like a Snorkosaurus to me!'

They saw Grandad asleep in his deckchair in front of the shed, snoring away.

'You're right!' said Vicky. 'It *is* a Snorkosaurus!'

'Hmmm,' Tom said. 'I think he's got ... um ...'

'Snorkosaurus sleeping sickness?' suggested Vicky.

'That's it!' agreed Tom.

Grandad began to wake up.

'Careful!' warned Vicky. 'A Snorkosaurus with Snorkosaurus sleeping sickness can be very dangerous!'

'Snorkosaurus?' asked Grandad who was now awake.

'Shhh,' Tom said. 'Snorkosauruses can't talk.'

'Ah, but I'm not a Snorkosaurus,' said Grandad. 'I'm a
Talkosaurus, and we're very good at talking. Very good indeed.'

Vicky giggled.

'Mind you,' continued Grandad, 'it's not all fun being
a Talkosaurus. I remember the time I had a set-to with an
enormous Tyrannosaurus Rex. He'd been pulling up my rose
bushes, and you know how I love my rose bushes ...

'... So I said to him, "You leave those rose bushes alone!"
Well, he turned round and gave me a very nasty look and
snorted down his great big nostrils. Then he stamped his foot
so hard that it made a huge hole in the ground – and that's
how I got my pond!'

'Well, Mr Talkosaurus,' said Tom, 'you're all better now.'

'I certainly am,' said Grandad. 'Thank you both very much. In fact, I feel so much better, I think I'm going to have a couple of nice, juicy human beans for my tea! Roaaarrr!'

Tom and Vicky ran away, laughing, and Grandad chased them round the garden until they were all out of breath.

Other Tom and Vicky titles available from Madcap

Chocks Away!
The Mow-Kay Corral

First published in Great Britain in 1999 by Granada Books, 76 Dean Street, London, W1V 5HA

Granada Books is an imprint of André Deutsch Ltd, in association with Granada Media Group

www.vci.co.uk

Tom and Vicky - A Wizard Animation Production for Granada Animation
© 1997 Granada Media Group Ltd
Licensed by Granada Media Consumer Products

Script adaptation by Loren Zeisler
Design by Traffika Publishing Ltd

A catalogue record for this title is available from the British Library

0 233 99645 1

Reprographics in the UK by Jade Reprographics
Printed in Belgium by Proost nv